THE STORM WHALE

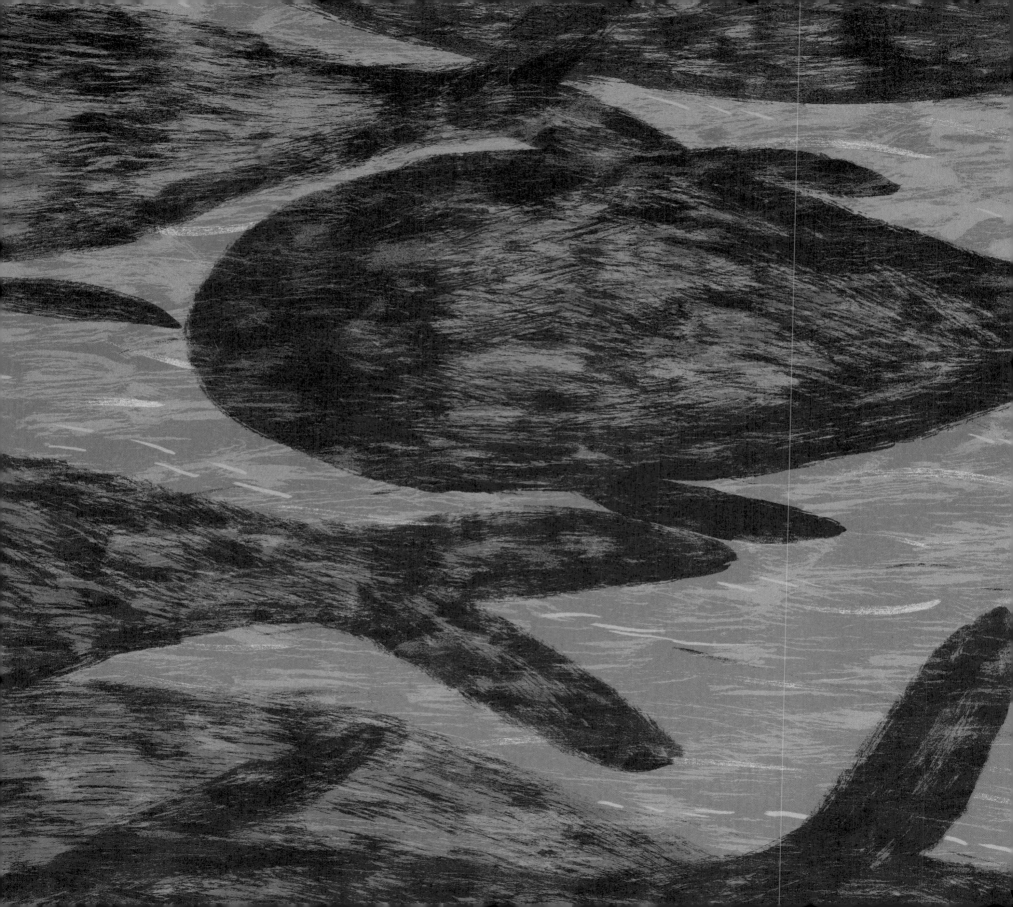

The wonder of the world
The beauty and the power,
The shapes of things,
Their colours, lights and shades,
These I saw.
Look ye also while life lasts.

SIMON & SCHUSTER
First published in Great Britain in 2013 by
Simon & Schuster UK Ltd, 1st Floor, 222 Gray's Inn Road,
London WC1X 8HB • This edition published 2023
Text and illustrations copyright © 2013, 2023 Benji Davies
The right of Benji Davies to be identified as the author and
illustrator of this work has been asserted by him in
accordance with the Copyright, Designs and Patents Act, 1988
All rights reserved, including the right of reproduction in whole
or in part in any form A CIP catalogue record for this
book is available from the British Library upon request
Printed in China • ISBN: 978-1-3985-2324-1 (HB)
ISBN: 978-1-3985-1963-3 (PB) • 10 9 8 7 6 5 4 3 2 1

THE STORM WHALE

Benji Davies

SIMON & SCHUSTER
London New York Sydney Toronto New Delhi

Noi lived with his dad and six cats by the sea.

Every day, Noi's dad left early for a
long day's work on his fishing boat.

He wouldn't be home again till dark.

One night, a great storm had raged around their house.

In the morning, Noi went down to the beach
to see what had been left behind.

As he walked along the shore,
he spotted something in the distance.

As he got closer, Noi could not believe his eyes.

It was a little whale washed up on the sand.

Noi wondered what he should do.

He knew that it wasn't good for
a whale to be out of the water.

"I must be quick!" he thought.

SOUNDS
of the
SEA
NDEL
VOL
II
WATERMUSIC

Noi did everything he could to make
the whale feel at home.

He told stories about life on the island.
The whale was an excellent listener.

The night was drawing in
and it was growing dark.

Noi was worried that his dad would be angry about having a whale in the bath.

Somehow, Noi kept his secret
safe all evening.

He even managed to sneak some
supper for his whale.

But he knew it couldn't last.

Noi's dad wasn't angry.
He had been so busy, he hadn't noticed
that Noi was lonely.

But he said they must take the whale
back to the sea, where it belonged.

Noi knew it was the right thing to do,
but it was hard to say goodbye.

He was glad his dad was there with him.

Noi often thought about the storm whale.

He hoped that one day, soon . . .

...he would see his friend again.

A Note from the Author

Ten years have passed since *The Storm Whale* was first published but it might surprise you to find out that its story is even older.

Some twenty years ago, my student animation project was about a little boy who found a whale on the beach and took it home to put it in the bath. I had always wondered if I could turn it into a picture book.

Many years later, as I walked along the shore in Whitstable, Kent, I stumbled across some old fishermen's huts. An ink sketch and some photos of those huts provided the perfect reference for a house by the sea. I wondered if it was the house where my whale-saving boy lived, so when I got home I set about creating the piece of artwork on the back of this book that is now so familiar to my readers. As I added the boy – at some point over the years I decided his name should be Noi – I imagined the breeze blowing off the sea, seagulls squabbling over scraps of fish, and a sentence drifted into my head:

"Noi lived with his dad and six cats by the sea…"

It felt like a beginning.

At the time, all I had wanted was to write and illustrate my own picture book. A decade later, the fact that *The Storm Whale* is still in print – alongside many more books that I have written and illustrated – and has been published in almost forty languages around the world, is beyond anything I could have dreamt. I am ever-thankful that my publishers at Simon & Schuster thought this story was worthy of becoming a picture book, as I had long hoped. In doing so, *The Storm Whale* helped me find a voice for my work as both author and artist.

Here's to Noi and his unfolding story.

Benji Davies
2023

More from the world of
THE STORM WHALE

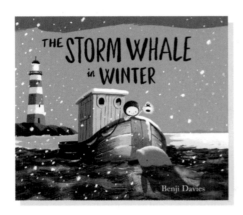

The Great
STORM WHALE
October 2023